Maple Tree Farm
BOOK TWO

Anna Helps Out

Chapter 1　A Big Help 2
Chapter 2　Strawberries 10
Chapter 3　Chores. 16
Chapter 4　Anna's Surprise 24

Written by Katherine Rawson
Illustrated by Steven Petruccio

Donated By
The Kiwanis Club
Of Arlington

PIONEER VALLEY EDUCATIONAL PRESS, INC.

Chapter 1
A Big Help

The morning sun was already bright
when Anna let the chickens into the yard.
"Here, chick, chick, chick," she called.
She tossed kitchen scraps from the bucket
in her hand. The birds clucked around her.

Anna smiled with satisfaction.
Just the other day, Aunt Polly
had said what a big help she was around the house.
"I don't know what we did before you came, Anna,"
she said. "In fact, I think you're ready
to have your own special chore.
How would you like to be in charge
of feeding the chickens?"

3

Anna felt as proud as the rooster in the barnyard. She had been at the farm only a few weeks and she was already taking care of the chickens.

"Next I'm going to learn to make butter and cheese. And I'm going to learn to grow vegetables and milk cows and . . . well, do everything on the farm!

Aunt Polly smiled. "You just worry about those chickens for now," she said.

Anna took her new responsibility
very seriously. But this morning
she was in a hurry to finish
because she planned to go strawberry
picking with her cousins, Harry and Sophie.

She had never picked strawberries before.
At home in Boston, they bought all their food
at the market. She wondered how strawberries grew.

"Anna! Come on!" Sophie ran by the chicken coop with a basket in her hand. "Hurry up!" she called and disappeared behind the barn.

Anna quickly dumped out the rest of the scraps. Then she hurried after Sophie with her white kitten, Ghost, at her heels.

When she rounded the barn,

she saw Harry and Sophie crouched

at the far end of the garden.

They were surrounded by rows of low green leaves.

"What are they doing?" she wondered.

She ran toward them.

9

Chapter 2
Strawberries

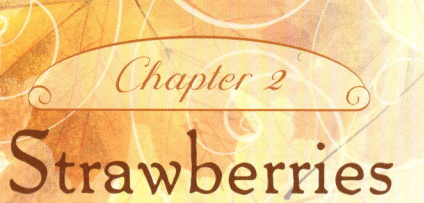

Anna plopped down on the ground next to Sophie and wiped her brow. "Where are the strawberries?" she said, looking around. "I don't see any."

"Look," said Sophie. She pulled aside some leaves to reveal a cluster of plump red berries. She bit into one. "Mmm," she said as red juice ran down her chin.

Anna picked a berry and took a cautious bite. It was warm and sweet. Juice stained her lips as she gobbled down the rest of the berry.

"The berries are supposed to go in your basket," said Harry, "not in your mouth."

But Anna saw a bit of red juice around his lips too.

"I'm going to pick lots of strawberries," said Sophie, "because Mama said she'd make us a special treat. I hope it's jam."

"Or strawberry shortcake," said Harry.

The children moved along the rows,
filling their baskets with fruit.
Ghost followed them,
chasing orange-and-black butterflies
through the plants.

Anna sat down to rest at the end of a row
and considered the contents of her basket.
"It's going to take all day to fill this," she said.
Then she noticed that Harry's and Sophie's baskets
were heaped high with berries.

"Don't worry," said Harry,
though Anna detected a little snicker in his voice.
"We've got plenty between the three of us.
Come on, I'll race you back to the house!"
He took off across the field
with Sophie following close behind.

Anna followed, but her feet dragged
under the heat of the sun.
When she reached the house,
Harry and Sophie were already sitting in the kitchen
drinking cups of cold water.

Chapter 3
Chores

Aunt Polly took Anna's basket and put it aside. "These berries look delicious," she said. She didn't seem to notice that the basket was only half full.

"Are you going to make strawberry jam? Please, please?" begged Sophie.

"We'll see." Aunt Polly smiled. "Anna, thanks for remembering to feed and water the chickens this morning," she said.

"Water? Oh no, I forgot that part!" said Anna.

"Don't worry," said Aunt Polly. "You can do it later. It takes practice to learn to do a chore well."

17

"I guess so," said Anna, looking at the floor.

"But I am learning, aren't I?" she said.

She looked up. "I'm going to learn

to do all the chores.

Even milking the cows."

"You?" said Harry. "Milk cows?

You can't even remember to water . . ."

Aunt Polly glared. "That's enough, Harry," she said.

"But Anna," she continued.

"Handling cows is hard work.

I don't think you're ready for something like that.

Maybe by the end of the summer."

Anna's face fell. "The end of the summer?"

"I think for now it's better to just watch Harry and Uncle Al," said Aunt Polly.

At milking time, Anna followed Harry to the barn. She watched Uncle Al bring the cows in from the pasture, and she helped open the barn door. Then she grabbed a milking stool and a bucket.

"You're supposed to watch," said Harry. "You don't know what you're doing."

"I've watched plenty of times," said Anna.
"I bet I can milk as good as you."
  She placed the stool next to a peaceful cow.
"I'm going to milk Daisy," she said.
"She's my favorite."

  She grabbed Daisy's teat and squeezed.
Nothing happened.

  Harry guffawed. "You have to pull down," he said.
"Like this." He stroked the teat,
  and a stream of warm milk squirted into the bucket.

"Oh, that's right," said Anna.

Her face turned red and hot. "I forgot."

She copied what Harry had done.

A lone drop of milk landed in the bucket.

"You have to do it harder," said Harry.

Anna squeezed harder.

"Moo!" bellowed Daisy.

She gave a kick with her rear foot

that knocked Anna off the stool.

Anna was stunned.

23

Chapter 4
Anna's Surprise

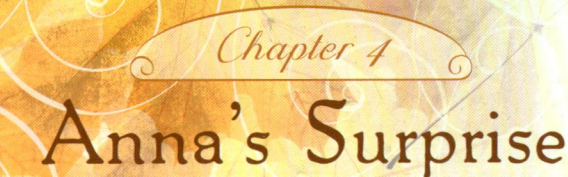

Anna stood up slowly.

Then, without looking at Harry,

she ran out of the barn toward the house.

She sat down on the back steps and tried not to cry.

"I can't do anything right," she moaned to herself.

"I can't water the chickens or milk a cow

or even pick strawberries right."

She didn't feel like the proud rooster anymore.

She felt like a little wet chick.

Anna sat on the steps for a long time.
When she didn't go inside at suppertime,
Uncle Al brought out a plate for her.

"Thanks," mumbled Anna without looking up.

"I have a favor to ask," said Uncle Al.

He set a wooden bucket down beside Anna.

"Turn this." He pointed to a crank attached to the top of the bucket.

"Keep turning and don't stop until I come back."

He went back inside the house.

Anna sat with her chin in one hand and turned the crank with the other.

"All I do around here is work, work, work," she muttered as she turned the crank.

"And still nothing turns out right."

With each turn, the crank felt harder to move. After a while, it took all her strength to move it. But she kept turning because Uncle Al had said not to stop.

27

Finally she heard Uncle Al behind her.
"Come inside," he said. "I have something
to show you." He took the bucket
and put it on the kitchen table.
The family gathered around.

Uncle Al took the top off the bucket.
Inside was something smooth and pink.
"Taste," he said, holding out a spoon.

"It's strawberry ice cream!" said Anna.

"I made it with the strawberries from your basket," said Aunt Polly.

"And you did all the hard work," said Uncle Al. "Turning that crank isn't easy, but you did it."

Anna smiled.

Everyone said that the ice cream was delicious
except Harry. He stayed silent,
but Anna noticed that he helped himself
to seconds and thirds.

"One day," said Anna,
putting down her empty dish,
"I'm going to milk the cow
and get the cream and make the ice cream
all by myself!"

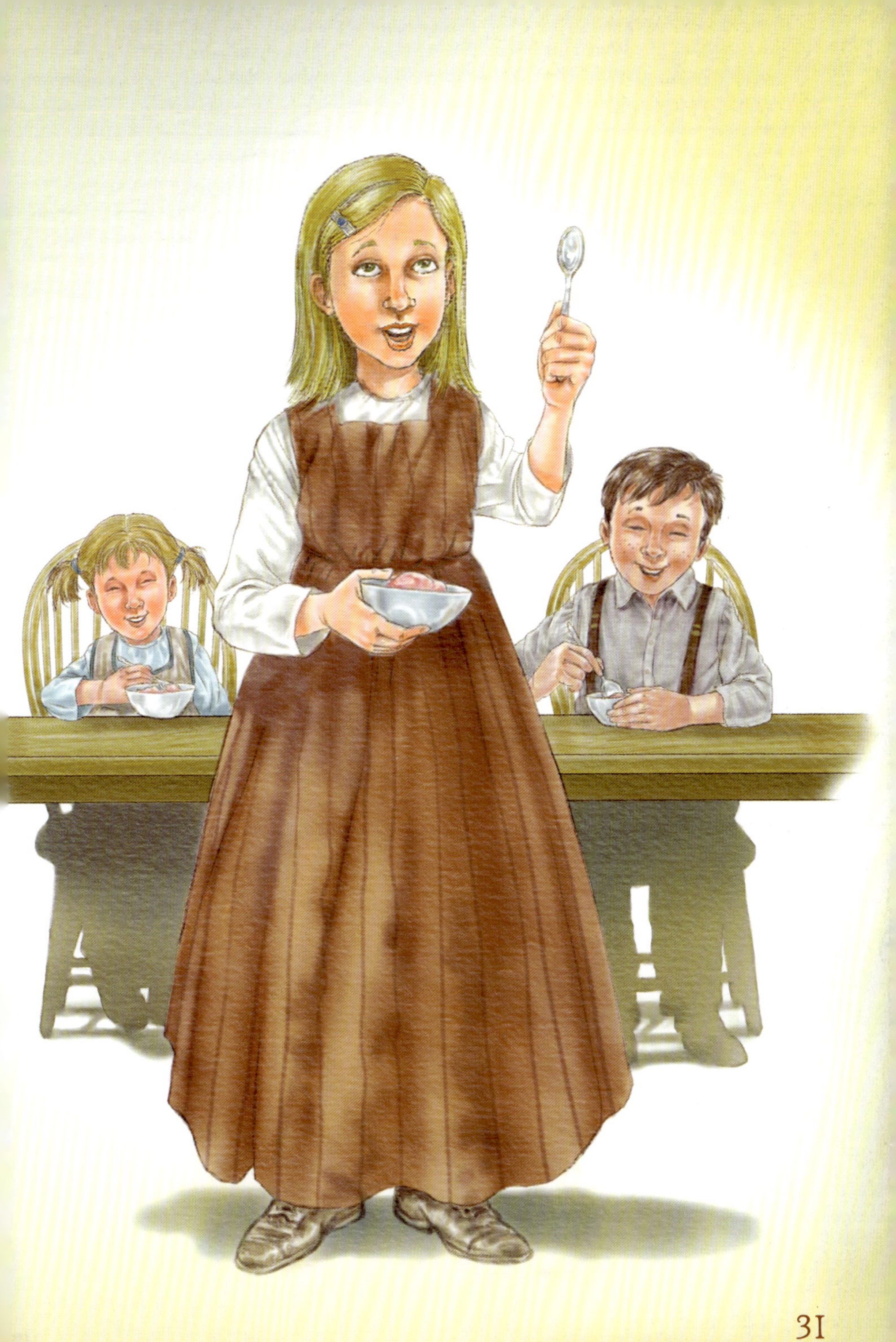

"I know you will," said Aunt Polly.

"You're already well on your way."